P9-CDS-652

EMMA AND THE SILK TRAIN

WRITTEN BY JULIE LAWSON

ILLUSTRATED BY PAUL MOMBOURQUETTE

KIDS CAN PRESS LTD.

"SILKER'S COMING!"

Emma ran to join her brother Charlie, drawn by the wail of the whistle, the billowing smoke and the rhythm of wheels rolling over the rails.

"Not so close!" Mama shouted from the station window.

Charlie grabbed Emma's hand and pulled her back.

Emma didn't mind. She was still close enough to feel the ground tremble as the silk train thundered past.

Emma's pa ran the station, so she knew all the trains. The only ones she cared about were the silkers — because hidden inside was a precious cargo of silk.

Pa said the silk came over the ocean all the way from China. It was so valuable silk trains rushed it across the country to New York, stopping only long enough to change crews and hook up a fresh engine with a full head of steam. Regular trains had to wait while the silkers sped through. Once, even a royal train was moved aside for a silker.

When Emma was five, Mama had fashioned a silk blouse for herself. Emma loved how it shimmered. There was enough silk left over for a hair ribbon for Emma and two squares for her patchwork quilt. But from that moment on, Emma longed for a silk blouse of her own.

2575

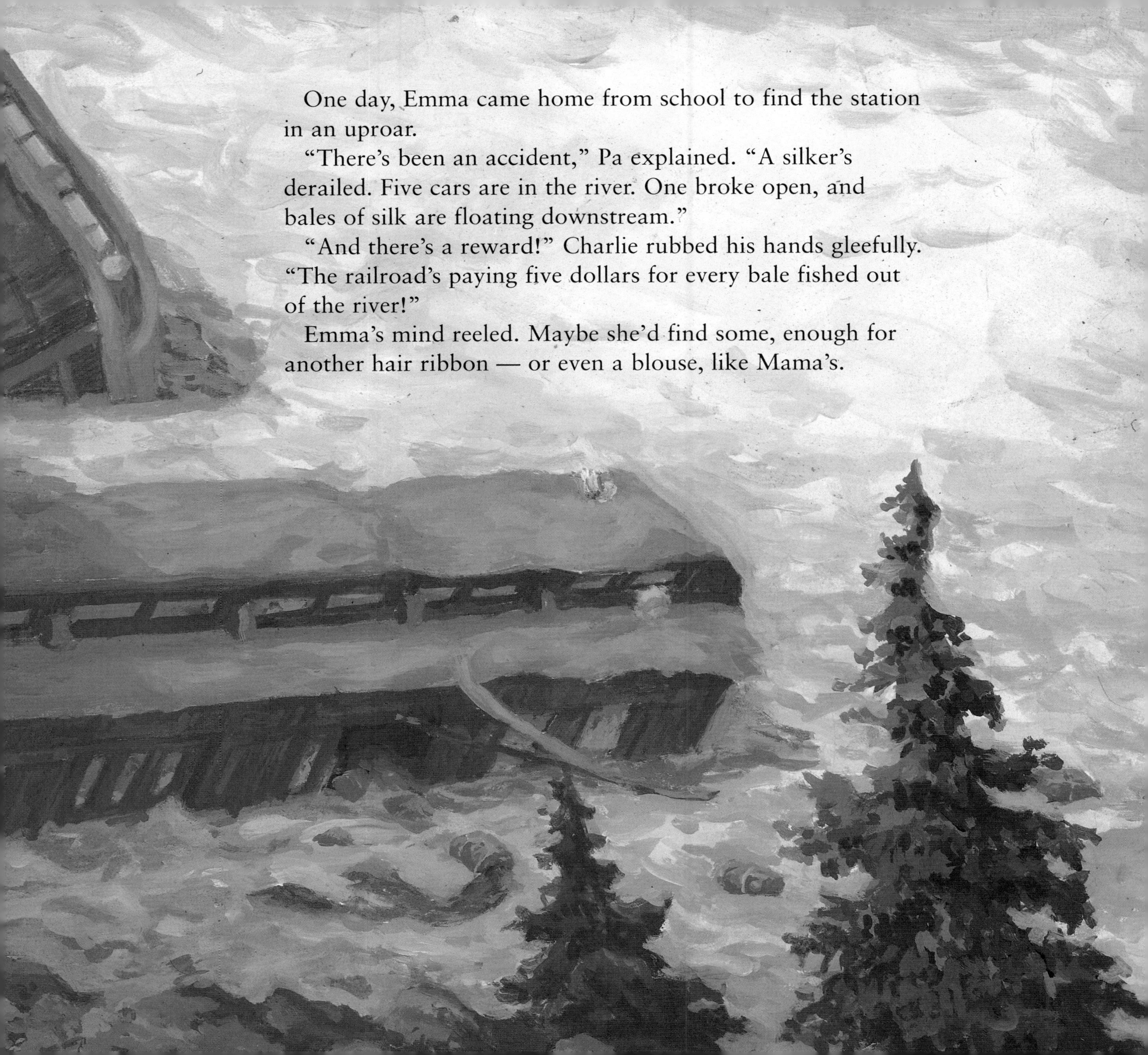

One day, Emma came home from school to find the station in an uproar.

"There's been an accident," Pa explained. "A silker's derailed. Five cars are in the river. One broke open, and bales of silk are floating downstream."

"And there's a reward!" Charlie rubbed his hands gleefully. "The railroad's paying five dollars for every bale fished out of the river!"

Emma's mind reeled. Maybe she'd find some, enough for another hair ribbon — or even a blouse, like Mama's.

The next morning, the whole town was fishing for silk.

By the end of the day, everyone had caught something.

A few people caught bales of raw silk.

Charlie caught a salmon.

Pa caught his fly-fishing hat, the one the wind had blown away the month before.

Mama caught a cold.

And Emma caught silk-fishing fever.

Long after everyone else had stopped, Emma kept fishing.

Sometimes she fished from shore.

All she caught was a gumboot.

Sometimes she fished from the wharf.

All she caught was a rusty kettle.

Sometimes she fished from the rowboat.

All she caught was disappointment.

"No more boat rides," Charlie decided one day. "Sorry, Emma, but it's been two weeks since the last silk bale was found."

But Emma didn't give up easily.

She searched the riverbank, in places where bales might be trapped by roots or partly buried in sand.

Still she found nothing.

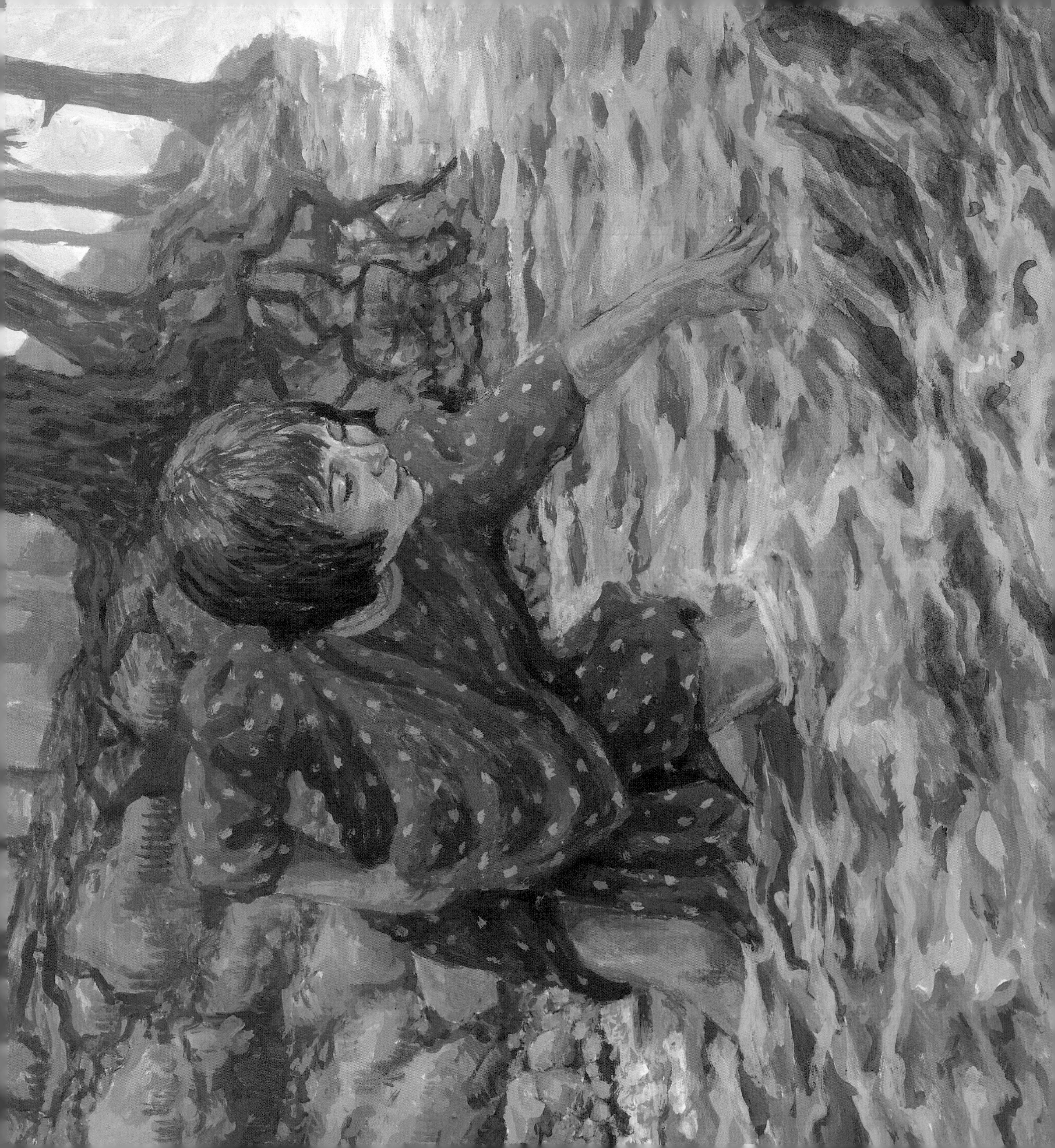

One afternoon, Emma's search took her farther than she was allowed to go. She was rounding the bend, promising herself she would head straight back, when she saw a splash of color a little ways from shore. The current caught the color and unfolded it into one long rippling stream. It looked red, until the sunlight touched it. Then it shimmered gold.

"Silk!" Emma cried. Enough for a blouse like Mama's — or even a dress! Quickly, she pulled off her shoes and stockings and hitched up her skirt. Bracing herself against the cold, she waded into the river.

The water licked at the hem of her skirt and swirled around her knees.

Just a few more steps —

Emma reached out and grabbed her prize.

Triumphant, Emma turned to go back. But at that moment the current tugged on the silk. Determined to hold on, Emma lost her balance. She gasped in panic as the river swept her off her feet.

Emma clutched the silk in her hand. She wouldn't let go. Not now! Gritting her teeth, she swam hard to reach the riverbank.

But she was no match for the current as it carried her farther and farther downstream.

Up ahead, Emma spotted a small island. Desperately, she fought the current as it threatened to pull her past.

She tried to touch bottom. Once, twice —

On the third try her toes grazed against something. Then her foot hit the muddy bottom.

She staggered to shore and collapsed in the sand. She had made it. And she still had her silk.

But as Emma looked at the fast-flowing water between her and the distant riverbank, she began to feel uneasy. How would she get off the island?

Wet and cold, Emma huddled against a log.

She scanned the riverbank, hoping to see someone, straining to hear a voice.

Silence. The bank was deserted.

The sun crept lower in the sky. Long shadows played tricks, making bushes and branches look like people waving from shore and walking along the tracks.

Tracks! The thought of them gave Emma an idea.

Standing on the log, she tied her silk so it flowed like a banner between two trees.

Then she waited.

Shadows grew longer. The silk snapped in the rising wind.

Emma rubbed her arms and stamped her feet to keep warm.

In the distance she heard a low, shaky rumble that swelled to a locomotive roar. A train burst around the curve. A silker!

Emma jumped up and down, waving frantically. “Help!” she shouted. “It’s me, Emma! STOP!”

But the train thundered past, vanishing in a cloud of flying cinders.

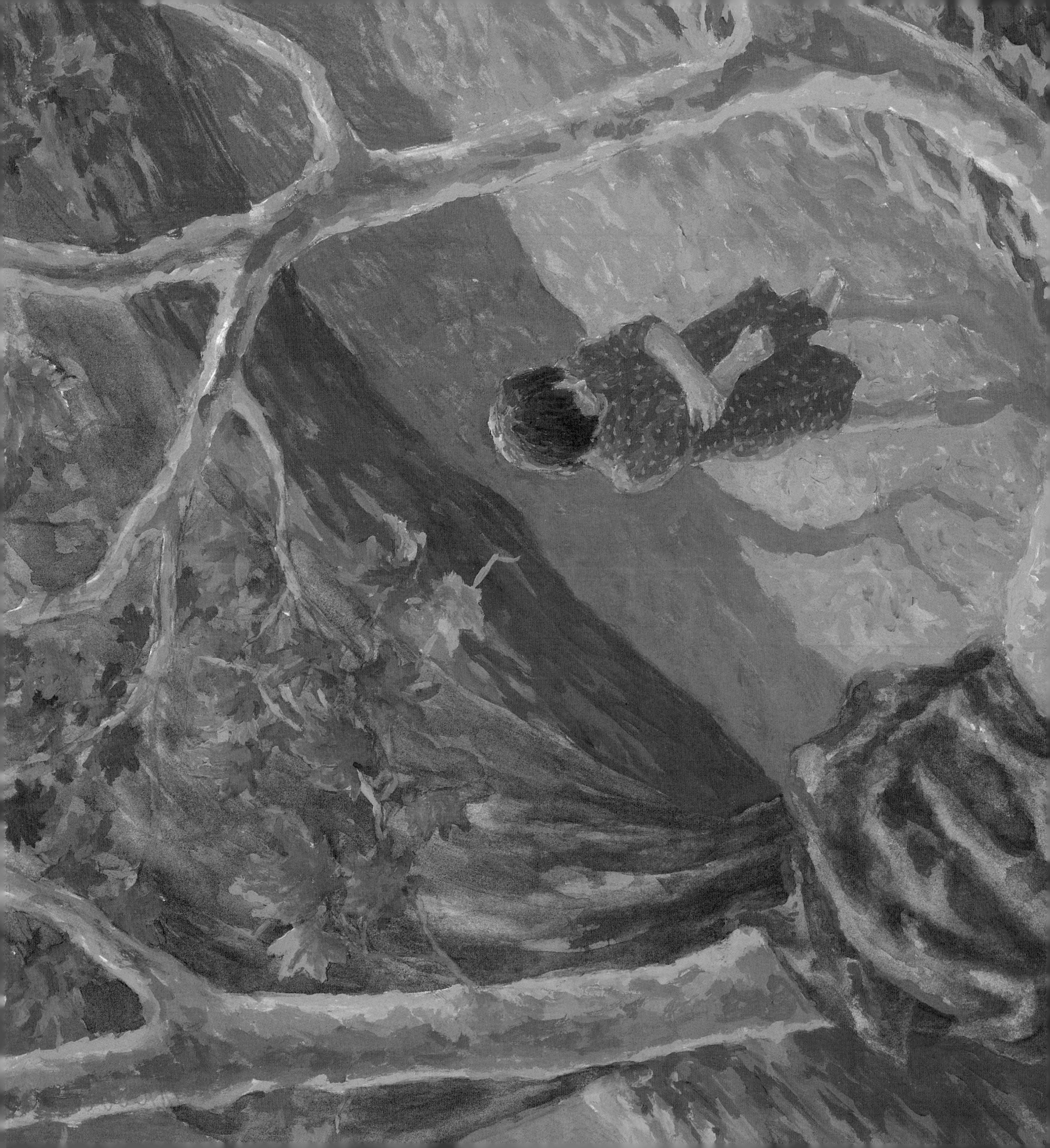

Emma swallowed hard. Silkers never stopped. Not for regulars, not for royalty, not for her.

The train's wailing whistle faded away, lost in the rush of the river, the sweep of the wind.

Emma waited. The sky turned black. One star appeared.

A westbound freight came into sight. Emma leaped to her feet and waved, but the train rumbled past.

A sob caught in her throat. *What if no one finds me?* she thought fearfully. *What if I'm here all night, all alone?*

She shuddered.

Then she heard it. Faintly at first, but growing steadily stronger. Voices calling. “EM-MA! EM-MA!”

Light flickered over the water.

“Mama!” she cried. “Pa! I’m here!”

Behind her, the silk caught the light and shone.

"Emma! Are you all right?" Mama hurried out of the rowboat and swept Emma into her arms. "We were so worried!"

"Oh, Mama!" Emma burst into tears. "I was afraid you'd never find me."

Mama wrapped Emma snugly in a blanket and wiped away her tears. "Thank heavens the crew on the silker spotted that banner you made. As soon as the train reached the station, the fireman swung down from the steps —"

"The silker *stopped*?" Emma was amazed.

Mama chuckled. "Not completely. Just slowed down enough for the fireman to hand your pa the message."

They were getting into the boat when Emma looked over her shoulder. "Where's my silk?" she cried out in alarm.

"Right here," Charlie said, placing it in her outstretched hands. "Boy, Emma. This is some catch."

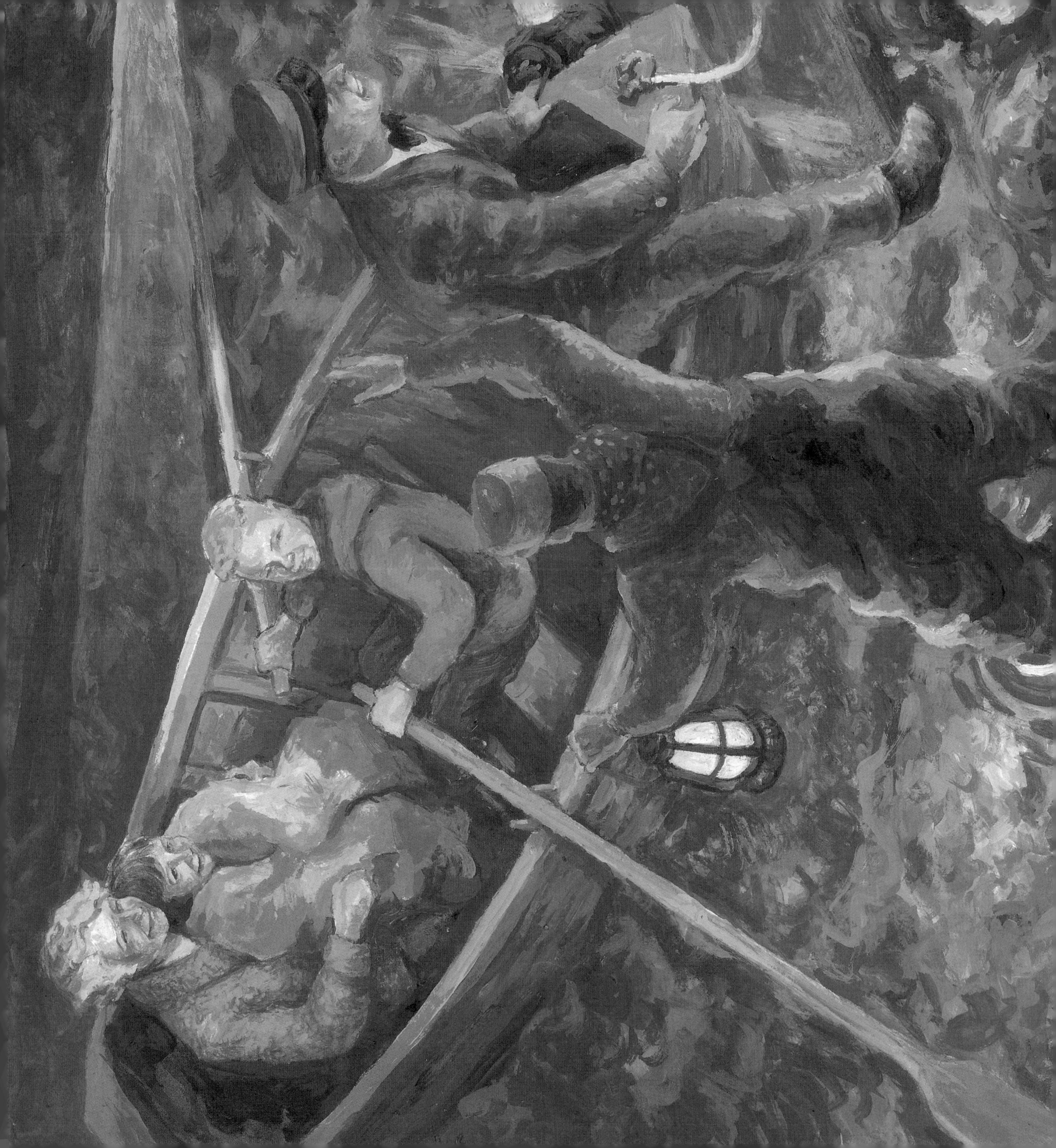

As Charlie rowed to shore, Mama turned to Emma and scolded gently. “You got a little carried away, fishing for silk. You know you’re not to go past the bend.”

Emma nodded. “I’m sorry, Mama.” She snuggled closer as Mama stroked her hair. “Will it be all right?” she asked.

Mama gave her a hug. “Now that you’re safe and sound? Of course.”

“I meant —”

“And the silk will be grand, you’ll see.”

Emma’s birthday came three weeks later.

Charlie eyed the cake hungrily. “Hurry up, Emma. Make a wish.”

“Listen!” she whispered. “Silker’s coming!”

A circle of light burst through the darkness. The whistle wailed as the train roared past the station.

Emma smiled. She didn’t need to make a wish. Her new silk dress rustled as she leaned forward to blow out the candles.

HISTORICAL NOTE

Emma and the Silk Train is based on an actual derailment that took place September 21, 1927, about 170 km (100 miles) east of Vancouver, British Columbia, along the Fraser River. Known as the "Million-Dollar Wreck," this derailment was the only major accident in the forty-year history of the silk trains.

The speed of the silkers was legendary. At ports on the west coast, bales of silk were transported from ship to train within minutes, and the silker was on its way. Onlookers kept a safe distance, afraid that the vacuum created by the fast-moving train might suck them under the wheels. And it was said that the last car of each silker was weighted down with iron to keep it from flying off the tracks. As the trains sped eastward, they set records for speed that have never been broken.

Why the speed? While traveling across the continent, the silk — both raw fibers and finished cloth — was insured by the hour, so the less time it spent in transit, the less it cost the shipper. The trains also carried cocoons of live silkworms, which were perishable.

By the end of the 1920s, the Panama Canal offered an all-water shipping route to the east coast. Silk trains gradually began to disappear, both in Canada and the United States. The Great Depression in the 1930s and the advent of synthetic fabrics sealed their fate. The last silk train crossed North America in 1941.

For my Anderson aunts, and my mom, who loved the trains — J.L.

To Maureen. Thank you for your love and support — P.M.

The author would like to thank the staff of C.P. Archives and the Revelstoke Railway Museum for their assistance during the writing of this book.

First U.S. edition 1998

Kids Can Press Ltd. acknowledges with appreciation the assistance of the Canada Council and the Ontario Arts Council in the production of this book.

Published in Canada by:	Published in the U.S. by:
Kids Can Press Ltd.	Kids Can Press Ltd.
29 Birch Avenue	85 River Rock Drive, Suite 202
Toronto, ON M4V 1E2	Buffalo, NY 14207

Edited by Debbie Rogosin and Trudee Romanek
Designed by Marie Bartholomew
Printed in Hong Kong by Wing King Tong Co. Ltd.

97 0 9 8 7 6 5 4 3 2 1

Canadian Cataloguing in Publication Data

Lawson, Julie, 1947–
Emma and the silk train

ISBN 1-55074-388-0

I. Mombourquette, Paul. II. Title.

PS8573.A94E45 1997 jC813'.54 C97-930402-4
PZ7.L38Em 1997